A Disappearing Act!

"We saw the prettiest butterflies at Flutter House today, Daddy!" Nancy said. "There was an orange one that landed on my shoulder and this big blue one called—"

Nancy stopped midsentence as she glanced up. There on TV was Josh. Standing next to him was Carmen!

"Daddy, Hannah, look!" Nancy said, pointing to the TV. "The people from Flutter House are on the local news!"

Nancy listened closely . . . .

"Flutter House is worried about our missing butterfly," Josh was telling the reporter, "especially since he's our only blue morpho."

Nancy almost dropped the dish she was holding. Did she just h   e heard?

"Morpho is missing way!"

Join the CLUE CREW
& solve these other cases!

NANCY DREW
AND THE CLUE CREW
#40

Butterfly Blues

BY CAROLYN KEENE

ILLUSTRATED BY PETER FRANCIS

Aladdin
New York London Toronto Sydney New Delhi

This book is a work of fiction. Any references to historical events, real people, or real locales are used fictitiously. Other names, characters, places, and incidents are the product of the author's imagination, and any resemblance to actual events or locales or persons, living or dead, is entirely coincidental.

6 ALADDIN

An imprint of Simon & Schuster Children's Publishing Division

1230 Avenue of the Americas, New York, NY 10020

First Aladdin paperback edition March 2015

Text copyright © 2015 by Simon & Schuster, Inc.

Illustrations copyright © 2015 by Peter Francis

All rights reserved, including the right of reproduction in whole or in part in any form.

ALADDIN and related logo, NANCY DREW, and NANCY DREW AND THE CLUE CREW are registered trademarks of Simon & Schuster, Inc.

For information about special discounts for bulk purchases, please contact Simon & Schuster Special Sales at 1-866-506-1949 or business@simonandschuster.com.

The Simon & Schuster Speakers Bureau can bring authors to your live event.

For more information or to book an event contact the Simon & Schuster Speakers Bureau at 1-866-248-3049 or visit our website at www.simonspeakers.com.

Designed by Karina Granda

The text of this book was set in ITC Stone Informal.

Manufactured in the United States of America 0416 OFF

10 9 8 7 6 5 4 3 2

Library of Congress Control Number 2014931010

ISBN 978-1-4814-1470-8

ISBN 978-1-4814-1471-5 (eBook)

CONTENTS

Butterfly Blues

CHAPTER ONE

Gotcha!

"This class trip is going to be awesome!" eight-year-old Nancy Drew exclaimed.

"Super awesome!" Bess Marvin agreed.

"Totally super awesome!" George Fayne added.

The three best friends were very excited to visit Flutter House, the cool new butterfly exhibit in their town. Thanks to their third-grade teacher, Mrs. Ramirez, their wish was about to come true!

"I heard there are hundreds of butterflies inside Flutter House!" Quincy Taylor said as the class followed Mrs. Ramirez to the Flutter House building.

"How do you think they got hundreds of butterflies in one place?" Nancy wondered as she brushed her reddish-blond bangs aside.

"Hundreds of butterfly nets!" Quincy joked.

Mrs. Ramirez stopped the class in front of the main entrance. The building was shaped like a caterpillar with a glass dome as its head!

"Today's a special day," Mrs. Ramirez said as they waited for their guide. "Does anyone know what it is?"

A few hands went up, but Antonio Elefano shouted, "It's Friday!"

Nancy rolled her eyes. Antonio was the class pest. He was always shouting before raising his hand.

"It's not just Friday!" Deirdre Shannon piped up. "Today is the first day of spring. Right, Mrs. Ramirez?"

"Correct, Deirdre," Mrs. Ramirez said with a smile.

But Antonio wasn't smiling.

"First day of spring!" Antonio mimicked

meanly. "Is that why you're wearing that goofy hat?"

Deirdre glared at Antonio under the brim of her big flowered hat.

"For your information," Deirdre snapped, "it's to remind everyone about my Mad Hatter Tea Party this Sunday."

Deirdre then turned to Nancy, Bess, and George and added, "Those who were invited!"

"Deirdre," Mrs. Ramirez warned. "Be nice."

Nancy, Bess, and George knew they weren't invited to Deirdre's party. Deirdre was always mad at the girls for something. This time she was mad at Nancy for getting the class job she wanted—watering the plants. Instead Deirdre got the worst job of all—cleaning the stinky turtle tank.

"Too bad we're not invited, Deirdre," George said. "I would have worn my favorite hat, too."

"You have a favorite hat?" Deirdre said, looking George up and down. George was wearing her usual faded jeans and a sweatshirt.

"Sure!" George said. She pointed to her dark curly-haired head. "My lucky ball cap with the mustard stain!"

"George!" Bess groaned, rolling her eyes.

Nancy giggled. She had been friends with Bess and George since kindergarten and still couldn't believe they were cousins. Bess was totally fashion forward. George was fashion *backward* and proud of it. Bess loved building gadgets. George loved gadgets too, as long as they were electronic. She loved her mom's minitablet, and she even was allowed to borrow it today!

Deirdre turned her nose up at the girls. She shifted her big tote bag on her shoulder, then walked over to her best friend, Madison Foley.

"I don't like tea anyway," Bess whispered, flipping her long blond hair.

"Hey, boys and girls!" a voice called out.

Everyone turned. A man not much older

4

than college-age was walking over. He wore a Flutter House polo shirt and a big smile.

"I'm Josh, your butterfly guide!" Josh said. "But before we check out some awesome butterflies—everyone must learn the butterfly wave!"

Nancy and her classmates copied the move Josh was doing. They pressed their hands together and waved their fingers like butterfly wings.

"Mrs. Ramirez, your class gets an A," Josh said. "Now, who's ready for a butterfly safari?"

"Me, me, me!" Harper shouted. She raised her hand high in the air while hopping up and down.

Nancy liked Harper, the new girl in class who loved butterflies. She wore a denim jacket with butterfly patches. And a different color butterfly barrette every day!

"I guess you like butterflies!" Josh said to Harper.

"I'm hatching some in my room, but they're not butterflies yet," Harper said. Her eyes lit up.

"Can I take some butterflies home? I'm sick of watching caterpillars!"

Josh shook his head. "You can't take any," he said. "But we have some toys and games in our gift shop."

"Like this?" George said. She pulled out the minitablet. "Check out this cool app I downloaded last night. It's called Butterfly Spy!"

Nancy smiled at the word "spy." She, Bess, and George weren't really spies, but they were detectives. They loved solving mysteries in their town of River Heights. They even had their own detective headquarters in Nancy's room.

"How does it work?" Josh asked.

"You just hold the tablet over a butterfly, click, and boom," George explained, "the name of the butterfly pops up on the screen."

"Neat!" Tommy Maron exclaimed.

"It is neat," Josh admitted. "But no electronics are allowed near the butterflies."

Josh then pointed to Antonio eating a big red apple left over from lunch.

"And no food, either," Josh said.

"Okay, okay," Antonio muttered. "I'll throw it away."

Everyone lined up while Josh opened the door. Nancy saw Antonio slip right behind Deirdre. She then saw something that made her frown. Antonio had dropped his half-eaten apple core into Deirdre's bag!

"I saw you put that apple in Deirdre's bag, Antonio!" Nancy said. "Take it out or I'll tell Mrs. Ramirez!"

"You better not!" Antonio warned before pushing his way to the front of the line.

"That apple is going to turn all brown and mushy in Deirdre's bag," Bess said, wrinkling her nose.

"Yeah," George said with a smile.

The girls forgot about Antonio as they filed into Flutter House. They followed Josh down a long hallway decorated with butterfly posters and mobiles. Also in the hall was the gift shop. Nancy could see fun butterfly toys and colorful butterfly-shaped pillows through the glass window.

"Cool!" Nancy exclaimed.

At the end of the hall was a room. When they were all inside, the kids looked around. Where were the butterflies?

"This room keeps the butterflies from flying outside the building," Josh explained.

"You mean escaping?" Tommy asked, wide-eyed.

"Don't worry," Josh said proudly. "No butterfly has ever escaped Flutter House!"

Josh walked to the back wall and lifted a curtain. "See for yourselves," he said.

Mrs. Ramirez's class filed through the curtain into another room. It was shaped like a dome and filled with—

"Butterflies!" Bess swooned.

Everyone started oohing and ahhing as dozens of colorful butterflies soared over their heads or rested on plants and flowers.

"It feels like summer in here!" Nancy said.

"Butterflies love warm weather," Josh explained. "That's why you see so many in the summer."

"What do butterflies eat, Josh?" Mrs. Ramirez asked.

"Most butterflies drink the nectar from flowers or fruit," Josh said.

"I knew that!" Harper declared.

A yellow-and-orange butterfly landed gently on Nancy's shoulder.

"Quick, Nancy!" Bess said. "Make a wish."

"Why?" Nancy asked.

"There's a saying that if you make a wish on a butterfly, it will come true!" Bess said excitedly.

"I *didn't* know that!" Harper admitted.

Nancy thought of some wishes but picked just one. She squeezed her eyes shut, then made her secret wish.

When Nancy opened her eyes, everyone was pointing to Josh. An even bigger butterfly had landed on his shoulder—a big blue butterfly!

"Wow!" Marcy Rubin said. "What kind of butterfly is that?"

"Meet our only blue morpho butterfly," Josh said.

"Morpho?" Peter Patino repeated. "Sounds like a superhero!"

"He's super, all right!" Josh smiled. "In fact, the morpho comes to us all the way from South America!"

"And now he's coming with *me*!" a woman's voice demanded. Then—

SNAP!

Nancy's eyes popped wide open as a sheer white butterfly net dropped over Josh's head and shoulders.

"Oh no!" Nancy gasped. "Who did that?"

CHAPTER TWO

News Flash

"Cheese and crackers!" Josh cried as he struggled to tear the net off his head. The blue morpho flitted around Josh's surprised face.

By now, everyone saw who was holding the net: a woman wearing a tan pantsuit and matching shoes.

"Who's she?" Bess whispered.

"It's Dorothy Danner the wedding planner!" George groaned quietly. "My mom catered some of her weddings, and she's bad news."

"Why?" Nancy asked.

"Whatever Dorothy wants, Dorothy gets!" George said.

"Looks like she wants that butterfly," Bess said.

Dorothy introduced herself to Josh and Mrs. Ramirez. She then pointed at the morpho.

"I'll take that butterfly, please," Dorothy said cheerily. "The bride and groom at my next wedding are planning a butterfly release after they say 'I do.'"

"Well, we don't give away our butterflies," Josh said, when he was finally freed from the net.

"But the bride needs something old, something new, something borrowed, and something *blue*," Dorothy explained.

Kendra Jackson stuck out her foot and said, "She can borrow my blue sneakers!"

Dorothy ignored her.

"I must have the butterfly," Dorothy told Josh. "It's my first outdoor wedding of the year!"

"Sorry," Josh said firmly.

"It's in the park . . . this Saturday . . . at three o'clock!" Dorothy went on.

"Good-bye, Ms. Danner," Josh said.

Dorothy frowned. She turned toward the curtain, but not before giving the morpho one last look.

"Uh-oh," Nancy whispered. "Something tells me she hasn't given up."

Everyone turned back to the butterflies. Excited chatter filled the dome, until Deirdre let out a big shriek.

"Help!" Deirdre cried as a flock of butterflies swarmed around her. "I'm being attacked!"

"They probably like the flowers on your hat," Josh pointed out.

"The flowers aren't real!" Deirdre said, waving her hands to swat away the butterflies. "They don't even smell like flowers!"

"It doesn't matter," Josh said. "Butterflies are attracted to the bright colors of flowers too."

"Well, we certainly learned a lot about butterflies," Mrs. Ramirez said. She smiled as she looked at her watch. "But it's two thirty and time to leave."

"Awww!" the kids groaned.

Nancy, Bess, and George didn't want to leave either.

"Good-bye, butterflies!" Bess said as the class followed Josh through the curtain.

"See you later, Morpho!" Harper called.

Later? Nancy glanced back at Harper. Was she planning to come back?

Her thoughts were interrupted as a smiling woman greeted them. In her hand was a feather duster.

15

"This is Carmen," Josh said. "She's going to dust you all off."

"Are we that dirty?" Quincy asked.

"It's not for dust, dear," Carmen said as she began dusting off Quincy. "It's to make sure butterflies haven't landed on your shoulders or heads."

"So they don't escape?" Marcy asked.

Carmen narrowed her eyes and said jokingly, "No butterflies escape Flutter House. Not on my watch!"

Dusted head to toe, Mrs. Ramirez's class boarded the big yellow school bus outside. Nancy, Bess, and George found empty seats.

"We were right, you guys," Nancy said. "This was an awesome trip."

"Super awesome!" Bess giggled.

Mrs. Ramirez began a head count. She stopped and said, "Why isn't Peter on the bus? Has anyone seen Peter Patino?"

"Here he comes!" Kendra said.

Nancy glanced out the window. Peter was running toward the bus. Clutched tightly in his hands was a paper bag.

"Peter, where were you?" Mrs. Ramirez scolded.

"Um—I had to get something," Peter blurted out. He slipped into the seat across from Nancy, Bess, and George. "Sorry, Mrs. Ramirez."

The bus began its trip back to River Heights Elementary School. Nancy glanced across the aisle at Peter. Her classmate smiled slyly as he peeked inside the bag.

"What's in the bag, Peter?" Nancy asked.

Peter glanced up from the bag. "Nothing!" he said quickly. "Zero, zip, zilch!"

Nancy shrugged at her friends. What was that all about?

"Boys!" Bess sighed.

"What do you get after you eat caterpillars?" Hannah Gruen joked in the kitchen later. Before Nancy could answer, she said, "Butterflies in your stomach!"

Nancy groaned even though the joke made her giggle. Hannah had been making Nancy giggle since she was three years old. That's how long Hannah had been the Drews' housekeeper and almost like a mother to Nancy.

"Good one, Hannah!" Mr. Drew chuckled as he turned on the small kitchen TV. "As long as caterpillars aren't for dinner tonight."

Nancy was setting the kitchen table. But all she wanted to do was talk about her awesome class trip.

"We saw the prettiest butterflies at Flutter

House today, Daddy!" Nancy said. "There was an orange one that landed on my shoulder, and this big blue one called—"

Nancy stopped midsentence as she glanced up. There on TV was Josh. Standing next to him was Carmen!

"Daddy, Hannah, look!" Nancy said, pointing to the TV. "The people from Flutter House are on the local news!"

Nancy listened closely . . .

"Flutter House is worried about our missing butterfly," Josh was telling the reporter, "especially since he's our only blue morpho."

Nancy almost dropped the dish she was holding. Did she just hear what she thought she heard?

"Morpho is missing?" Nancy said slowly. "No way!"

CHAPTER THREE

M Marks the Spot

Nancy moved closer to the TV to hear more.

"Do you think the blue morpho butterfly flew out of the building?" the reporter asked Josh.

"Never," Josh said, shaking his head. "Butterflies never escape Flutter House!"

"Not on my watch!" Carmen added.

"Then what happened to it?" the reporter asked.

"It's a mystery!" Josh said with a shrug. "The last visitors we had today were a third-grade class."

"We were the last ones there," Nancy said, "but not the *only* ones."

"Who else was there?" Mr. Drew asked.

"A wedding planner named Dorothy Danner," Nancy answered. Her eyes lit up. "She wanted the blue morpho for a wedding she is planning."

"I think I know what you're thinking, Nancy," Hannah said. "That Dorothy Danner might have stolen the butterfly?"

"She did have a butterfly net!" Nancy remembered.

"That doesn't sound good," Mr. Drew agreed.

"Could someone please drive me to Flutter House?" Nancy asked. "So I can tell Josh it was Dorothy who took Morpho?"

"Whoa!" Mr. Drew said with a smile. "You know a good detective needs clues before blaming anyone."

Nancy knew her father was right. He wasn't a detective, but he was a lawyer. And lawyers knew a thing or two about mysteries and cases.

"And who knows?" Mr. Drew went on. "While you look for clues, you might find more suspects."

"True, Daddy," Nancy agreed. "But I'm pretty

21

sure the butterfly thief was Dorothy Danner."

As Nancy went back to setting the table, she said, "I'm also sure of something else."

"What?" Mr. Drew asked.

"That this is a case for the Clue Crew!" Nancy declared.

The next day was Saturday. The Clue Crew gathered that morning in Nancy's room to work on the case. Before they could start, Bess wanted to demonstrate her latest invention . . .

"It's a foldable butterfly net!" Bess said proudly. "If we find Morpho, I just pull it out of my pocket, unfold it, and *gotcha*!"

"You mean *when* we find Morpho, Bess," Nancy said. "You know the Clue Crew never gives up."

"Then let's get to work!" George said. She sat down at Nancy's computer to open a new case file. "What do we know so far?"

Nancy paced back and forth across her shaggy rug. She always thought best that way.

"We know that Morpho went missing yesterday afternoon," Nancy said. "And he probably didn't fly out on his own."

"How could anybody take a butterfly out of Flutter House?" Bess asked.

"Especially with Carmen dusting us off like we had cooties!" George added.

"Unless," Nancy said slowly, "someone came back later to take Morpho—when Carmen and Josh were busy or weren't looking."

"Okay, but who?" Bess wondered.

"Dorothy might have come back," Nancy said. "She did look at Morpho funny before she left."

George began their suspect list with Dorothy Danner. When she was finished typing, she asked, "Who else could have taken Morpho?"

"Someone who wanted a butterfly," Bess decided. "*Really* wanted a butterfly."

"Harper Novak!" Nancy exclaimed. "She wanted to take a butterfly home. Before we left, I heard Harper say, 'See you later, Morpho!'"

"Write Harper's name, George!" Bess said.

"I am, I am," George said, typing quickly.

"Two suspects but only one clue," Nancy said. "Let's go back to Flutter House and look for more."

George found the Flutter House website. It was open on Saturdays and Sundays from eleven thirty to four o'clock.

"Flutter House, here we come," Nancy said. "And I hope we find lots of clues!"

"I hope we won't get dusted again," Bess said with a frown. "That feathery thing tickles!"

24

CHAPTER FOUR

Clue-in-the-Box

It was eleven thirty when Hannah drove into the Flutter House parking lot. While Hannah sat in the snack hut, called the Caterpillar Café, the girls headed straight to the Flutter House building.

"Remember," Nancy said, "we have to meet Hannah outside the cafe in a half hour. So let's work fast."

When Nancy, Bess, and George reached the ticket booth, they frowned. Tickets for the butterfly dome were eight dollars each!

"We don't have eight dollars!" Nancy groaned. "How are we going to go inside?"

"We can pretend we lost something," George

said. "That excuse always works for us!"

The girls rushed to the ticket booth, where a teenage girl sat. Stitched on her polo shirt was the name "Sophie."

"You can't go inside without a grown-up," Sophie said.

"We don't want to go inside!" Bess said. "I mean—we do want to go inside, but not to look at butterflies."

"But it's a butterfly habitat," Sophie said. "What else is there to look at besides butterflies?"

"We were here on a class trip yesterday," Nancy said quickly. "And I lost my—"

"—Watch!" Bess finished.

"You're wearing a watch," Sophie said, nodding down at the purple watch on Nancy's wrist.

"Um—I wear a watch on each wrist!" Nancy blurted.

"She likes to have a lot of time on her hands!" George joked. "Get it?"

Sophie didn't chuckle. She reached down and pulled up a big cardboard box.

"What's that?" Nancy asked.

"Our lost and found," Sophie explained. "You can look for your watch in here."

The girls traded disappointed looks. All they wanted to do was go inside Flutter House!

"But—" Nancy started to say.

"Each item is tagged with the time and place it was found," Sophie explained. "I found most of the stuff. I'm great at lost and found!"

"Thanks," George muttered, taking the box.

The girls pretended to look through the lost items. There were three wool hats, two hoodies, a bunch of gloves, and—

"Someone's retainer?" Bess said, wrinkling her nose. "How gross is that?"

"Let's give this box back and try to get inside," George said.

Suddenly Nancy spotted something sparkly. She pulled it out. It was a gold butterfly-shaped barrette. On it were the initials *HN*.

"*HN* for Harper Novak!"

Nancy pointed out. "It's one of Harper's butterfly barrettes!"

"So?" George said. "She probably lost it yesterday during the class trip."

"Harper was wearing a *pink* barrette yesterday!" Nancy said. "Not a gold one."

"She could have been here weeks ago," Bess said.

Nancy turned the barrette over in her palm. On the back was a tiny sticker with the date and time the barrette was found.

"The barrette was found yesterday at four o'clock!" Nancy said.

"What does that mean, Nancy?" Bess asked.

"Maybe Harper came back after school yesterday," Nancy said, "to take Morpho!"

"Why would she be wearing a different barrette?" George asked.

"Doesn't everybody change their clothes after school?" Bess asked.

"Everybody but me!" George argued.

Nancy, Bess, and George returned the lost

and found box to Sophie, but not the barrette.

"May we take this barrette, please?" Nancy asked. "We know who lost it."

Sophie raised an eyebrow. "How do I know you don't just want a pretty sparkly butterfly barrette?" she asked.

George folded her arms. "And how do we know you're so great at finding things?" she asked.

"What do you mean?" Sophie asked.

"You didn't find the missing blue morpho butterfly, did you?" George demanded. "Well, did you?"

Sophie blinked a few times. She then waved her hand at the barrette as if to say, *Take it.*

"Thank you!" Nancy said. She pocketed the new clue. Then she, Bess, and George headed for the Caterpillar Café.

"That Sophie was a tough nut to crack," George complained. "What next?"

"Cookies at the Caterpillar Café!" Bess declared. "I heard they're shaped like butter-flies."

"But after cookies, we find Harper Novak," Nancy said. "And hopefully Morpho!"

It was a little after noon when Hannah dropped the girls off near Harper's house. They weren't sure where the Novaks lived. Only that their new house was near Bess's.

"I sometimes see Harper riding her bike up and down this block," Bess said as they looked around. "It's a pink bike covered with butterfly stickers."

"Surprise, surprise," George joked.

After a few more steps, Nancy saw a sign taped to a tree. It read: MAKE YOUR WISHES COME TRUE!

Pasted on the sign were a butterfly sticker and an arrow pointing up the block.

"Let's see where it leads," Nancy said.

The girls headed straight up the block until they found another sign, also decorated with butterfly stickers. This one read: WISHES AROUND THE CORNER!

Nancy, Bess, and George turned the corner to

see another sign taped to a tree: MEET THE BUTTER-FLY WHISPERER!

"What's a butterfly whisperer?" Nancy whispered.

"And what do they whisper to butterflies?" Bess whispered.

"I don't know," George said. "But why are *we* whispering?"

Suddenly they heard voices. Nancy, Bess, and George turned to see a bunch of kids lined up in front of a house.

THE GREAT BUTTERFLY WHISPERER

"What are they lining up for?" Nancy wondered.

"It can't be for lemonade," Bess decided. "It's still too cold."

The girls neared the house. They could see a small table at the end of the line. Sitting behind the table was Harper. On top of it was a sheer net cage. Inside was . . .

"A blue butterfly!" Nancy gasped.

The girls traded excited looks. They knew of only one blue butterfly, and that was Morpho!

ChaPTER FiVE

Caterpillar Chiller

Nancy, Bess, and George walked toward Harper and the caged butterfly. Until Henderson Murphy shouted, "Hey! No jumping the line."

"This is business," Nancy explained.

"Detective business!" Bess added.

Marcy Rubin's little sister, Cassidy, was the last in line. The six-year-old folded her arms and said, "Business-shmizness. Even detectives have to wait their turn!"

"Okay, okay," Nancy said as they stepped behind Cassidy. "What's everybody lined up for, anyway?"

"That new girl from school has a wishing

butterfly!" Cassidy said, pointing to Harper. "I'd tell you my wish for a real-live pony, but then it wouldn't come true."

"Riiight," George said slowly.

Nancy's eyes had already lit up. Did Cassidy say a wishing butterfly?

"Harper saw me make a wish on the orange butterfly," Nancy told Bess and George. "Maybe she wanted a butterfly to make wishes on."

"Or for other kids to wish on," Bess said.

"Why would she want Morpho?" George asked. "Wouldn't any butterfly be good enough?"

"Morpho was the biggest butterfly in the butterfly dome," Bess said. "Big butterfly—big wishes."

Nancy tried to be patient as they inched closer to Harper and the blue butterfly.

"Listen, everybody!" Harper told the crowd. "Be ready to write down your wish when you get to the table."

"Why should I give my wish to you?" a girl called from the middle of the line.

"So I can whisper it to the butterfly!" Harper said, pointing to the cage. "That's why."

"Why can't we whisper our wishes ourselves?" another girl asked.

"Because," Harper said, her face beginning to turn red, "I'm the Butterfly Whisperer, that's why!"

Cassidy raised her hand. "But if you see my wish for a real-live pony it won't come true!" she said.

"And aren't you supposed to free the butterfly after every wish?" a tall boy with glasses asked. "No wish will come true with it cooped up in that dumb cage!"

Harper's face was tomato red as she stood up. She slammed her palms on the table, making the butterfly cage jump.

"Whatever, okay?" Harper cried. "I'm sick of all this complaining!"

She picked up the cage, turned toward the house, and said, "Find some genie to tell your wishes to. I quit!"

"No!" Nancy, Bess, and George said at the same time. They had to get a look at that blue butterfly before they lost their chance.

The butterfly cage swung from Harper's hand as she climbed the front steps of her house.

"Wait, Harper!" Nancy called.

Too late. With a slam of the door, Harper and the blue butterfly were inside the house.

The Clue Crew ran to the door. Nancy knocked, and after a few seconds it was opened by Harper's mom.

"Hi," Mrs. Novak said with a smile. "You must be Harper's new friends."

Nancy, Bess, and George nodded their heads.

"Her room is right upstairs," Harper's mom said, pointing up a staircase. "The one with the butterfly sign on the door."

"Thank you, Mrs. Novak!" Nancy said.

The Clue Crew bounded up the stairs to Harper's room. The door was open a crack, so they peeked inside.

"I don't see Harper," Nancy whispered.

"Or the butterfly cage," Bess asked.

"I'm going in," George said, opening the door wider.

"George," Nancy hissed. "Wait—"

George was already inside the room. She sighed at the butterfly pillows on Harper's bed and the butterfly-stitched curtains on her window.

"Doesn't she ever get sick of butterflies?" George asked, shaking her head. "What's wrong with dogs or cats or hamsters—"

"Look!" Bess said. She pointed to a glass tank on Harper's desk. "It's filled with fuzzy caterpillars!"

"Harper told us she had caterpillars," Nancy said as she peered inside the tank. "They're fuzzy, all right."

"Did Harper ever say she had a *giant* caterpillar?" George asked slowly.

"Giant?" Nancy repeated. She looked to see where George was pointing and gulped. In the back of the room, lying still against the wall, was a super-sized caterpillar!

"Omigosh—it's as big as me!" Bess squeaked.

The Clue Crew stood frozen, staring at the caterpillar. Until it squirmed, and they screamed!

"Eeeeeek!"

A head popped out of one end of the caterpillar. It was Harper's head!

Harper pulled a set of earbuds out of her ears. "Nancy? Bess? George?" she said. "What are you doing in my room?"

"Your mom let us up here," George said. "Didn't you hear us?"

"I was listening to music," Harper said, holding up the earbuds. "I heard you scream, though."

"What were you doing inside that thing?" Bess asked.

"It's my awesome caterpillar sleeping bag," Harper said. She crawled out and stood up. "I snuggle in it and listen to music when I'm sad."

"Why were you sad?" Nancy asked.

"Because my Butterfly Whisperer table was an epic fail!" Harper groaned.

"Where is the butterfly now?" Bess asked.

"Here," Harper said. She pulled aside the curtains. On the windowsill was the butterfly cage. Inside was the blue butterfly!

"Where did you get it?" Nancy asked.

"It's my first butterfly to hatch!" Harper explained proudly. "Pretty cool, huh?"

Nancy wanted to run straight to it, but Harper kept talking. . . .

"It's not easy being the new kid at school," Harper said. "That's why I made myself the Butterfly Whisperer. To make new friends."

"Is that why you took Morpho, too?" George asked.

"Morpho?" Harper asked, surprised. "I heard

he was missing, but why would I take him?"

Nancy pulled the butterfly barrette from her pocket.

"We found this at Flutter House today," Nancy explained. "It was lost there right after our class trip."

"So that's where I lost it!" Harper exclaimed. "The gold one is my favorite barrette."

"So you did go back to Flutter House after school?" Nancy asked.

"I went back with my mom," Harper said. "I wanted to show her all the neat butterflies."

Harper then frowned and said, "But they closed early because of a missing butterfly."

"Then where did you lose the barrette?" Bess asked.

"Probably at the Caterpillar Café," Harper said. "It was still open, so my mom and I went there for cookies."

"Cookies, huh?" George said. She lifted an eyebrow. "What are they shaped like?"

Harper looked at George as if to say, *Duh.*

"They're shaped like butterflies!" she said.

"Could be a lucky guess," George whispered to Nancy and Bess.

Nancy studied Harper. Was she telling the truth? Had she lost her barrette in the café, and not in the butterfly dome?

"While you're here," Harper said with a grin, "do you want to see my fuzzy caterpillars?"

George pointed to the blue butterfly on the windowsill. "We'd rather see *that*!" she declared.

Nancy, Bess, and George raced to the sheer white cage and looked inside. The butterfly was blue.

"This one is smaller than Morpho," Nancy said.

"He's a lighter color, too," Bess added. "How do we know if it's a blue morpho?"

"Here's how," George said as she pulled her mom's minitablet from her jacket pocket. She opened the Butterfly Spy app, held the tablet over the cage, then clicked the button.

"Is it a morpho?" Nancy asked.

George turned the tablet over and looked at the screen. "Nope," she said with a frown. "In fact . . . it's not even a butterfly!"

Nancy's eyes popped wide open. *Not a butterfly?*

CHAPTER Six

Take the Cake

"I heard that, George!" Harper said. "What do you mean it's not a butterfly?"

"It's a moth!" George answered. "This thing identifies butterflies *and* moths."

Nancy, Bess, and Harper huddled around George's tablet to read the screen.

"It says: blue tiger moth," Nancy confirmed.

"It's a moth, all right." Bess sighed.

Harper groaned under her breath.

"I can't believe it!" Harper cried. "I thought my grandparents sent me a *butterfly*-hatching kit!"

"Didn't you read the box?" George asked.

"I didn't think I had to." Harper shrugged. "I thought I knew everything about butterflies."

Harper pointed to her caterpillar tank. "Great," she grumbled. "In just a few days my room will be swarming with moths!"

"Moths can be pretty," Bess said.

"Just don't let them near your sweaters," George added.

Nancy felt bad for Harper. All she wanted to do was make friends.

"I have an idea, Harper," Nancy said. "Why don't you join the Bug Club?"

"Bug Club?" Harper repeated.

"Some kids from school meet once a week to talk about bugs," Nancy explained. "Some even bring their bugs to the meetings."

"You can bring your butterflies," George said, then quickly added, "I mean . . . moths."

"And you can make new friends, too," Nancy said.

Harper seemed to give it thought. "I guess butterflies are bugs," she said. "Flying bugs with wings."

"I guess," Nancy said, although she didn't like to think of them that way.

"Thanks for telling me about the Bug Club," Harper said. She then turned to the windowsill. "Would you like to make a wish on my . . . moth?"

"Yeah!" George sighed. "I wish we would find Morpho already!"

Nancy, Bess, and George left the Novak house.

"Our only suspect is Dorothy Danner the wedding planner," Nancy said.

"Dorothy told Josh she had an outdoor wedding today," George remembered. "And they're freeing a bunch of butterflies."

"She said the wedding is in the park," Bess said. "At three o'clock, I think."

Nancy glanced down at her watch. "It's almost two o'clock now," she pointed out. "We have plenty of time to make it."

"Yippee!" Bess cheered. "We're going to a wedding!"

The girls ate a quick chicken sandwich lunch at Bess's house. They then headed straight to the park.

Nancy, Bess, and George all had the same rules. They could walk anywhere as long as it was no farther than five blocks away, and as long as they were together.

When they reached the park, they glanced around. They saw the playground, dog run, and basketball court, but no wedding.

Suddenly Nancy, Bess, and George heard soft music in the distance. They followed the music to the prettiest part of the park. The big open field was surrounded by yellow and white daffodils and neatly trimmed hedges.

"What's that for?" Bess asked. She pointed to a huge white tent set up in the middle of the field.

"That's where the wedding guests eat and dance," George said.

Nancy saw chairs lined up on both sides of a long white satin runner. Guests were taking their seats on both sides of the aisle. At the end of the aisle was a gazebo decorated with flowers.

"That's where the bride will walk down!" Nancy said. "But where are the butterflies?"

Nancy, Bess, and George moved closer to the chairs. They looked up the aisle to see a small table set up next to the gazebo. On top of the table was a pretty white cage. Inside the cage were . . .

"Butterflies!" Bess gasped.

"One of them is blue!" George pointed out. "I can see it from here!"

A boy walked over to the butterfly cage. He held a camera over it and snapped a picture.

"I want to get a better look too!" George said.

Just as the girls were about to walk toward the butterfly cage, the music grew louder. Nancy turned to see a parade of bridesmaids in pink dresses walking toward the aisle.

"Not now, George," Nancy said. "The wedding is starting!

"Pretty!" Bess swooned as the bridesmaids filed down the white satin runway.

"Pretty *annoying*!" George muttered. "Now we have to wait until the bride and groom free the butterflies!"

Next came a flower girl tossing rose petals from a basket. She was followed by the bride, led down the aisle by a proudly smiling man. Nancy guessed it was her dad.

Nancy, Bess, and George stood behind the chairs, watching the wedding. As the bride and groom read their vows, George whispered, "What's taking them so long? 'I do' is just two little words—"

"Shh!" Nancy hissed.

The couple finally said "I do." They walked over to the cage, then opened the door together. Everyone began to ooh and ahh as the butterflies flew out into the air.

"There's the blue one!" Nancy pointed out. "Bess, did you bring your butterfly net?"

"One butterfly net," Bess said, holding it up. "Check!"

"Let's get Morpho!" George declared.

The Clue Crew kept their eyes on the blue butterfly. It swooped over the guests' heads and into the big white tent. Nancy, Bess, and George raced inside too.

"Where did he go?" Nancy asked.

The girls looked around.

Tables were set with snowy white tablecloths, delicate china, and crystal glasses. White-jacketed waiters carefully filled each glass with water.

"There he is!" Bess said.

Nancy and George looked to see where Bess was pointing. In the back of the tent stood a towering wedding cake decorated with pink icing swirls and sugar roses. The blue butterfly hovered over the cake. Then it delicately landed on top.

"Come on!" George said.

As Nancy, Bess, and George rushed toward the cake, a waiter shouted, "Hey, now! Where are you girls going?"

The Clue Crew stopped in front of the wedding cake and the butterfly.

Bess held up the butterfly net with both hands. Instead of bringing it down, she froze!

"What are you waiting for?" George cried. "Bring down the net, Bess!"

"But it's a wedding cake!" Bess wailed, holding the net midair.

"And it's so beautiful!" Nancy agreed.

"Give me that!" George demanded. "I'll try to be careful!"

George grabbed the net from Bess's hands and held it over the cake. But before she could drop it . . .

"Stop!" a woman's voice shouted.

The girls whipped around.

Dorothy Danner the wedding planner was racing into the tent. Her high-heeled shoes clicked on the dance floor as she charged forward.

"Don't you dare!" Dorothy warned, waving her arms. "Don't you dare touch that cake!"

ChaPTER SEVEN

Pest Quest

Nancy, Bess, and George watched sadly as the blue butterfly fluttered away and out of the tent.

"Now we'll never get him." Nancy sighed.

"A butterfly chase?" Dorothy asked. She pointed to the net in George's hand. "That's not what I had planned for this wedding!"

"Unless it was a blue morpho butterfly?" George asked.

"What are you talking about?" Dorothy demanded.

"Did you go back to Flutter House yesterday, Ms. Danner?" Nancy asked. "For that butterfly you wanted?"

"We were on the class trip yesterday," Bess explained. "We saw how much you wanted the blue morpho."

"You think I stole the butterfly?" Dorothy asked. "I did nothing of the kind!"

"So you didn't go back?" Nancy asked carefully.

"Absolutely not," Dorothy huffed. "After I left Flutter House, I went straight to a meeting with my staff."

The waiters nodded their heads in agreement.

"Then where did you get the blue butterfly?" Bess wanted to know.

"I caught it myself," Dorothy said.

"With your net?" George asked.

Dorothy shook her head.

"I found the butterfly earlier today on the fruit platter," Dorothy explained. "The pineapple chunks, to be exact."

Pineapples!

"Josh said butterflies love fruit," Nancy

whispered to Bess and George. "They drink the juice."

"When I saw the butterfly, I grabbed a water glass," Dorothy went on. "I quickly turned it upside down over the butterfly, and it was mine!"

"Oh," Nancy said. But was Dorothy telling the truth?

"Now," Dorothy said narrowing her eyes, "why don't you girls be like pretty little butterflies—and *take off*?"

Nancy, Bess, and George left the wedding tent. Once outside they began talking all at once.

"I don't know if I believe Dorothy!" Bess said.

"Even if she did catch it," George said, "that butterfly still could have been Morpho!"

"I wish there was a way to find out," Nancy said. Her eyes lit up when she saw the boy who took the picture of the butterflies in the cage.

"Excuse me!" Nancy called. "Can we see the picture you took of the butterflies?"

"How come?" the boy asked as he walked over.

"Um . . . because butterflies are pretty!" Bess said.

"That's not why I took the picture," the boy said. "I want to be a nature photographer when I grow up."

"Awesome," George said. She nodded at the camera still in his hand. "But are you any good?"

"Way good," the boy said. "See for yourself."

He found the butterfly shot in his camera. As he showed it to the girls, he said, "I got a neat shot of the blue one."

The Clue Crew studied the picture of the blue butterfly. It was blue, like Morpho, but not totally.

"This one has gold spots on its wings," Nancy said.

"Morpho never had gold spots." Bess sighed.

"Do you want to see my picture of a water bug?" the boy asked next. "I found it under the sink—"

"No, thanks!" the girls said at the same time.

The boy shrugged, then hurried toward the tent. As they walked away, Nancy said, "Morpho is still missing and we have no suspects."

"Maybe we'll have better luck tomorrow," Bess said, forcing a smile.

As the girls left the park to head home, they noticed a flier taped to a tree. It was for a kid magician named Presto Peter.

"Hey—it's Peter Patino!" Nancy said, pointing to the magician's picture. Peter was wearing a magician's cape and top hat.

George leaned forward to read the flier: "Meet Presto Peter on Sunday at noon. Watch him perform his awesome butterfly trick."

"Butterfly?" Bess said. "Where did Peter get a butterfly?"

Nancy thought back to the class trip and how Peter ran onto the bus with a paper bag.

"Bess, George," Nancy said, "do you think Morpho was in the bag Peter was holding?"

"He wouldn't tell us what was inside," George said.

"Maybe because Morpho was in the bag!" Bess gasped.

Nancy gave the flier another look. The word "butterfly" was written in big *blue* letters. Blue like Morpho!

"What are we going to do, Nancy?" Bess asked.

"We are going to see that butterfly tomorrow!" Nancy declared. "Before Presto Peter makes it disappear!"

ChaPTER EighT

AbracaNABra!

Nancy, Bess, and George knew where Peter lived, so on Sunday they headed straight to his house.

Mr. Patino opened the front door and smiled.

"I guess you're here for the magic show," Mr. Patino said. "It's right downstairs in the basement."

The girls ran down the stairs. Down in the basement were more kids, some from school. Quincy, Marcy, Cassidy, and Kendra sat on folding chairs. They faced a table covered with a starry tablecloth.

Nancy, Bess, and George sat in the last row, next to one another. They stretched their necks to study the things on the table.

"A deck of cards, a rubber chicken, a book," George said. "But where's the butterfly?"

"Where's Peter?" Nancy wondered.

Everyone jumped as a microphone screeched.

Peter's voice announced in a deep voice, "And now, the Patino Magic Lounge in majestic River Heights proudly presents . . . Presto Peter!"

"Yay!" little Cassidy cheered.

Peter stepped out from behind a large flat-screen TV. He was wearing his magician's cape and top hat. He whipped his cape back with a flourish, bowed, then stood behind the table.

"For my first trick I'll need a volunteer," Peter said with a big grin. "Can I please have a volunteer from the audience?"

"What's a volunteer?" Cassidy shouted.

"A helper," Marcy hissed to her little sister.

"I'll do it," Quincy said, jumping up. He walked behind the table where Peter stood. "Okay, what do I have to do?"

"Just answer my question," Peter said. "Did you get your allowance today?"

"Nope," Quincy said.

"Oh, yes, you did!" Peter declared. He reached his closed fist to Quincy's ear. He then opened his hand to reveal a quarter. "Ta-daaa! Here it is!"

"Neat," Quincy said. "But my allowance is three dollars a week."

Peter frowned at Quincy. "You can sit down now," he said.

Quincy shrugged, pocketed the quarter, then returned to his seat. Peter turned back to the audience and said, "Do I have another volunteer for my next trick?"

"Go ahead, Nancy!" Kendra said.

"Yeah, Nancy," Marcy urged.

"Okay, okay," Nancy said. She stood up and joined Presto Peter behind the table. "What should I do, Peter?"

"There's a page in this book I'd like you to read," Peter said as he handed Nancy the book. "Open it right at the bookmark."

"Sure," Nancy said.

But when she opened the book to the marked page . . .

Whoosh!

Something blue fluttered out and into the air. It moved so fast it was a blur, but Nancy was sure it was one thing: a butterfly!

"Bess, George!" Nancy cried. "Help me out!"

"Hey!" Peter shouted as the girls jumped up and down under the butterfly. "What do you think you're doing?"

"We know what that is, Peter," George said, stretching her arm up.

"And we want it!" Bess said.

"Well, you can't have it," Peter said.

Peter took off his hat and used it to scoop up the butterfly. He then flipped the hat and the butterfly upside down on the table.

"This trick is over!" Peter said as he pressed down hard on the hat. "Please return to your seats, ladies and gentlemen!"

Nancy narrowed her eyes at Peter.

"It's not over," Nancy said, "until you pick up that hat and show us the butterfly!"

ChaPTER NiNE

Fruity Factoid

"We know you have a butterfly under that hat, Peter," George said. "Let us see it."

"No!" Peter snapped.

"What's so special about a butterfly?" Quincy asked.

"The blue morpho butterfly is missing from Flutter House," Nancy explained.

"I heard about that!" Kendra said.

"Me too!" Marcy said as she stood up. "Maybe the missing butterfly *is* under Peter's hat!"

"Come on, Peter," Quincy said. "Show us the butterfly already!"

The kids began walking toward the table.

"Stand back!" Peter shouted. "Presto Peter never reveals the secrets of his tricks!"

"Wait a minute," George said. She cupped her hand behind her ear as she leaned toward the table. "There's a noise under the hat."

The room became quiet as everyone listened. Nancy listened too. What she heard was a muffled whirring noise.

"Butterflies don't make that sound," Nancy said.

"Nancy, George!" Bess called from the other side of the room. "I just found the bag Peter had on the bus!"

"Great," Peter muttered.

Nancy, Bess, and George looked inside the bag. They thought it was empty until Nancy found a sales receipt. It was from the Flutter House gift shop.

Nancy read the receipt aloud: "One wind-up butterfly, blue."

"Is that what's under the hat, Peter?" Kendra said. "A toy butterfly?"

"We thought it was the real deal!" Quincy complained.

"Wellll," Peter said with a shrug, "it looks real . . . doesn't it?"

Peter lifted the hat. Underneath was a blue plastic butterfly. It gave one last flutter before sputtering to a stop.

"Show's over." Quincy sighed.

The other kids left. Peter frowned as he was left alone with the Clue Crew.

"I couldn't tell you the butterfly was a fake!" Peter insisted. "What magician gives away his tricks?"

"I know, Peter," Nancy said. "We were just trying to find Morpho."

"How are you going to find a missing butterfly, anyway?" Peter scoffed.

"What do you mean?" Nancy asked.

"Butterflies can fly far away," Peter answered. "Morpho can be anywhere by now!"

Nancy didn't want to think about that. All she wanted was to find Morpho!

The Clue Crew said good-bye to Peter, then left the Patino house.

"Peter might be right," George said. "Morpho could have flown anywhere by now. Another town, another state—even another country!"

"Do you think we should give up?" Bess asked softly.

"No!" Nancy said, shaking her head. "As I said, the Clue Crew never gives up."

"Okay." George sighed. "But I wish Peter really was a magician—so he could make Morpho magically appear!"

The Clue Crew returned to Nancy's house. After eating Hannah's homemade soup for lunch, they hurried upstairs to their headquarters.

"Now we really have no more suspects or clues," Bess said. "What next?"

"Maybe Flutter House posted something about Morpho," George said. She opened the Flutter House website. There was no news about Morpho, but something else to see . . .

"There's our class picture from the trip on Friday!" Nancy said excitedly.

The girls smiled when they saw the picture of Mrs. Ramirez's class on the website. The caption read, "Third-Grade Flutter Fans."

"I don't see me," Bess said, studying the picture.

"You're hidden by Deirdre's hat." George laughed. "And those super-sized flowers!"

"Flowers!" Bess gasped. "Remember how the butterflies swarmed around Deirdre's hat?"

"So?" Nancy asked.

"So maybe Morpho escaped on Deirdre's hat," Bess said.

Nancy gave it a thought, then shook her head.

"Carmen dusted Deirdre's big flowered hat for butterflies," Nancy explained. "I saw her myself."

George found a butterfly list on the website. She clicked on "blue morpho." A picture of the blue morpho butterfly appeared. So did fun facts about the butterfly.

"It says the blue morpho likes to drink the juice of rotten fruit and mud!" George said.

"How can something so pretty be so gross?" Bess cried.

"Rotten fruit is pretty gross," George agreed. "Did you ever see how fast an apple core turns brown and mushy?"

Rotten fruit . . . apple . . . brown and mushy?

Nancy's jaw dropped as she remembered the apple core in Deirdre's bag. The one Antonio dropped inside!

"Nancy, what's up?" George asked.

"You guys," Nancy said slowly, "maybe Morpho didn't escape on Deirdre's hat. Maybe he escaped inside her *bag*!"

ChaPTER TEN

Spy a Butterfly!

"Hurry up!" Nancy called as the Clue Crew raced down the block. "We can't miss Deirdre's Mad Hatter Tea Party!"

"I don't get it, Nancy," George called. "Even if Morpho was in Deirdre's bag, wouldn't he have flown out by now?"

"Then he's somewhere in the house!" Nancy called back.

"We can't search Deirdre's whole house, Nancy!" Bess wailed. "We weren't even invited to her party!"

The Clue Crew reached the Shannon house, one of the biggest houses in River Heights. As they walked up the path, Nancy whispered, "I hear voices in the back."

Nancy, Bess, and George rounded the house to the backyard. Sitting around a picnic table were Deirdre and some girls from school. On the table were cookies, cupcakes, and a pretty pink-and-white teapot.

All the guests wore hats. Deirdre wore her big flowered one. When she saw Nancy, Bess, and George, she frowned and said, "What are you doing here?"

"Show us your bag, please, Deirdre," Nancy

said. "The one you brought to Flutter House on Friday."

"My bag—why?" Deirdre demanded.

"We want to look for the missing butterfly from Flutter House," Nancy explained. "Antonio Elefano put a—"

"I don't care if you're looking for buried treasure!" Deirdre said. "You're not snooping in my bag!"

The girls stared at Deirdre. Things didn't look very promising, until Bess blurted out, "If you let us look, Nancy will switch class jobs with you!"

Nancy turned to Bess and said, "I will?"

"You mean Nancy will clean the turtle tank?" Deirdre asked slowly. "And I'll get to water the pretty plants?"

"I guess," Nancy said through gritted teeth.

"Do it, Deirdre!" Andrea Wu urged.

"That turtle tank stinks worse than my brother's socks!" Kayla Bruce said.

"Deal!" Deirdre declared. She pointed to the

house. "I dropped my bag in the laundry room on Friday."

"The laundry room?" Bess asked, confused.

"I came in through the side door," Deirdre explained. "The laundry room was the closest place to leave it."

As the girls raced toward the house, Deirdre called, "And don't take my books out. I didn't start my homework yet!"

Nancy, Bess, and George opened the side door. Sure enough, the laundry room was right inside.

"There's Deirdre's bag!" Bess said, pointing. "It's on top of the washing machine."

The girls stood on tip-toe around the washing machine and the bag. George pulled the bag open and—

"Pe-ew!" Bess cried.

George reached in and pulled out the apple core. It was dark brown and mushy. "Applesauce anyone?" she teased.

"Where's Morpho?" Nancy asked.

The girls dug through Deirdre's bag. They found three books, a feathery pen, and a panda-face change purse.

"No blue morpho, or any butterfly." Nancy sighed.

She was about to close the bag, when George said, "That's what you think."

Nancy turned toward George and gasped. Perched on top of her head was a big blue butterfly!

"He flew in front of my face and up to my head!" George exclaimed. "Am I lucky or what?"

Startled, the butterfly flew off George's head. It landed on top of a detergent bottle on the floor.

"It looks like Morpho," Bess said quietly.

"But is it Morpho?" Nancy whispered.

"Let's see," George said as she pulled out her minitablet. Very quickly she opened the Butterfly Spy app.

"What does it say?" Nancy whispered as George held the tablet over the butterfly.

"It says . . . blue morpho!" George said softly.

"Omigosh, omigosh!" Bess whispered. "It's him!"

Using her foldable butterfly net, Bess gently scooped up the morpho. As the girls turned to leave the laundry room, they saw Deirdre and her friends at the door.

"Is that Morpho?" Deirdre asked, pointing to the sheer butterfly net in Bess's hands. "How did he get in here?"

"I tried to tell you, Deirdre," Nancy said. "Antonio dropped an apple core in your bag on Friday. Blue morphos eat rotten fruit, so—"

"Ewww, gross!" Deirdre cried. "Get that flying insect out of here!"

"Gladly, Deirdre," Nancy said. She turned to her friends. "Come on, Clue Crew—let's bring Morpho home!"

The girls rushed the blue morpho back to Nancy's house. Then Hannah drove them directly to Flutter House.

Josh and the rest of the staff were thrilled to see the morpho again, and grateful, too.

"Flutter House can't thank you girls enough," Josh told the Clue Crew inside the butterfly dome. "We thought we'd never see our blue morpho again."

"It's a good thing he liked rotten apples!" George said with a grin.

Josh left to give Hannah a tour of Flutter House. The girls strolled through the dome, watching the butterflies.

"What did you wish for on Friday, Nancy?" Bess asked. "When the pretty orange butterfly landed on your shoulder?"

"Yeah, Nancy," George urged. "Spill!"

Nancy smiled. She knew wishes were supposed to be secret, but nothing was a secret among best friends. . . .

"Okay," Nancy said. "I wished that the Clue Crew would be the most awesome detectives ever!"

"And guess what?" George said as they watched the morpho happily flitting from flower to flower. "I think your wish came true!"

When spring is in the air, so are butterflies! Now with this cool and super-easy craft, you can have fun with butterflies all year round.

Things you'll need:
sheets of tissue paper in different colors
1 clothespin
paint or markers
1 pipe cleaner
scissors
glue
2 googly eyes (optional)

Directions:
Use markers or paint to color the clothespin. This will be the butterfly's body.

Paint on a face or glue on googly eyes!

For the butterfly's wings, cut tissue papers in oval shapes.

Stack the ovals on top of each other.

Bunch papers together in the middle. Next, clasp the middle with the clothespin.

Show off the colors by fluffing out the tissue paper wings.

Fold the piper cleaner into a V-shape. Curl the ends to make the butterfly's antennae.

Glue the antennae to the top of the clothes-pin "head."

Craft more butterflies for a whole fluttering flock!

HAPPY SPRING!

Nancy Drew and the Clue Crew®

Test your detective skills with more Clue Crew cases!

Visit NancyDrew.com for the inside scoop!

From Aladdin · KIDS.SimonandSchuster.com

Mermaid Tales

*Exciting under-the-sea adventures
with Shelly and her mermaid friends!*

Break out your sleeping
bag and best pajamas. . . .
You're invited!

Sleepover Squad

❋ Collect them all! ❋

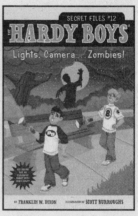

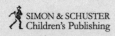